The Adventures of

Firstyr the Younger

Knight Errata of Cort

BED TIME STORIES FOR YOUNG LAWYERS

STORIES BY
EDWARD PONTACOLONI

ILLUSTRATIONS BY
ROBERT PLACE

To order additional copies of this book, contact:
Xlibris
1-888-795-4274
www.Xlibris.com
Orders@Xlibris.com

CONTENTS

FIRSTYR UNCOVERS A RUSE, OR
THE NEW EMPEROR'S CLOTHES

Long ago, in the faraway land of Cort, lived the dullard King Meenot the XII. King Meenot was not blessed with the wisdom for which wiser kings are renowned, and there was a lot of discontent and dissent in his kingdom. The day ultimately came when King Meenot convened the Cort Council of Peals to address the problem of the widespread dissension.

Now, the Council of Peals was comprised of former Kings, which explains why Meenott was the XII and not the II or even the VIII, and the Council knew very well the extent of the dissent in the kingdom, much of which was aired in the Council halls. The Council determined that much of the problem was attributable to the fallibility of the King, and that the solution thus simply lay in decreeing that the King was infallible. They knew, however, that such a decree would not be readily received by the people unless they could eliminate some of the realm's more vocal critics. However, these malcontents first had to be properly identified.

The Council decided to declare a day of loyalty, and to hold a royal parade to mark the occasion of their declaration. The plan was to parade the King throughout the realm, escorted by disguised secret agents and census-takers. These loyal servants would determine which citizens failed to attend the festivity, and they would identify those in attendance who voiced dissent. Once known, all dissenters would be arrested as suspected non-believers and imprisoned for as long as necessary to convince the remaining populace that the King was indeed infallible, as decreed.

For the parade, the King desired to wear the finest robes, and the services of the realm's great clothiers were solicited. Most were ostensibly too busy, but, one Pandophe, a famous tailor, who also owned a used car dealership, ultimately answered the call.

Now this Pandolphe was no fool, but the King most certainly was, and Pandolphe schemed to take advantage of the situation. It seems that Pandolphe was also a closet dissenter, but his service to the King enabled him to escape detection.

Pandolphe suggested to the King that, although the parade was a good idea and all, it didn't have much chance of success. He explained that everyone was aware of the hidden purpose of the parade, so that even the most ardent dissenters planned to attend, but to keep their voices still.

Pandolphe had a better idea. He would make the King fine clothes of the sheerest fabrics; materials that could only be seen by persons who were trustworthy and loyal to the King, the real "true believers." Thus, anyone who should fail to see the King's robes might be immediately exposed as untrustworthy and disloyal. The fabrics would be very expensive, and the tailor would command a very high price, but, the King was prepared to spare no cost in

order to be infallible.

As we all know, such fabrics do not exist, but, Pandolphe easily deceived the King with a tailoring pantomime, and none of the King's counselors or attendants dared to challenge the ruse for fear that they would be thought disloyal if they could not see the fabrics.

So it was that the King ended up parading down the streets of Cort in his birthday suit. However, Pandolphe had forewarned the people, and no one dared to say a word. No one, that is, except for a young squire from another kingdom, Firstyr the Younger, whose youthful innocence and naiveté caused him to freely exclaim, for all to hear, that the King was truly stark naked.

The misguided youth was immediately apprehended, shackled and dragged before the Council of Peals. Head bent, he was berated by the Chief Councilor. "Dare you to challenge the infallibility of our King! His right is divine! His word is law! What say you in your defense?"

Firstyr humbly spoke. "Honorable Council, I come from another land where old Pandolphe also worked his wizardry. There he connived and gave witness and convinced our infallible Emperor that the song of a mechanical bird was the equal to that of our endangered nightingale, whereupon the Emperor authorized the destruction of a forest to put up condominiums. Where once we thrilled to melodious bird song, we are now left with only the cacophony of a wind-up toy. Had our appeals only been heard! Shall the land of Cort suffer a similar fate?"

"Dare you!" the Chief Councilor demanded, "Do we not know our own best interests? The findings and pronouncements of our King must not be subject to retrial in our halls lest there be no peace. We demand certainty and finality. Peace demands it, and the habitat of a songbird would be just as small a price to pay in Cort as it was in your land."

"Away with him! Banish him from Cort!"

And the youth was led away, banished to the dreary lands of the Tranactionalists.

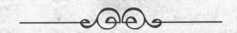

FIRSTYR RESCUES A DAMSEL LOST FOR WORDS,
OR THE ALLUSION ILLUSION

Thus, our young hero was exiled to the land of Corporate, where he labored amongst the Transactionalists. There, against the wicked Warefors and the heinous Hirtafors he did battle the vile monsters of the dreaded Legalese. His early deeds gained him great renown as, with his vorpal sword, forged in the furnaces of White Mountain, he warranted and defended the lands of the titled nobility. His adventures were made song, and he was legend.

So it was that the day came when he was summoned to the castle of his liege, the Duke Senexatty. Said the Duke, "My brave young Firstyr, I have great need of your skill and courage. My daughter and her entourage appear to have become lost in the Allusion Swamp, and we have not had word of them for longer than we can abide."

"The Allusion!" interrupted the troubled Firstyr, "But . . ."

"Listen," commanded the Duke, who resented the interruption, but held his royal temper in deference to his gallant squire's youth, whose immature tendency to blurt had been forewarned in his deportation from Cort.

"Alluvio Maris!" said Firstyr to himself, without revealing the fear that was welling up inside him.

"Come here," said the Duke, as he spread his maps on the table before him. "Here," said the Duke, marking the lines of a darkened region with his finger, "the Allusion mires an area of unsurveyed square hectares, with boundaries measured in rods and chains between ancient trees and weathered stones. It would be impassable except on flat boats with long poles pulled by strong arms. But, long ago my forebears cleared and filled a passage along this route," and he traced the way with his finger, "an easement that we have maintained, by force of arms when necessary, to serve our dominant estate. Along this route my daughter and her troop should have been able to pass through the Allusion unmolested. Wandering afar would have entailed great risk and unknown perils."

"The vile monsters of Legalese?" wondered the knight aloud.

"A war, even a war of words, is still a war," replied the Duke.

Placing his hand upon Firstyr's shoulder, the Duke led the young knight away from the map table to a balcony vista overlooking the expanse of his estate and beyond to the horizon, in the direction of the Allusion Swamp. "Find and rescue my daughter, young Firstyr," pled the Duke, the hint of a tear in his eye. "Take a troop of my elite Paras, fully armed, stout and true, and leave at once, for more time must not be lost."

Genuflecting, with his hand on the hilt of his sword, Firstyr acknowledged his office and made oath to his task. "My free act and deed," he swore. Then he rose, turned, and with cautious pride he took his leave. "Ebba et fluctus," he thought to himself.

He made his exit through a hall adorned with the portraits and the trophies and the

prizes of generations of Senexatties: the silver cup of the Joust of Moot; the many gilt plaques awarded for victories in the Tribulations; the jewel encrusted grail awarded for the Supreme Contention; and he slowly shook his lowered head in the sad surmise that such awards might never be his.

Out in the courtyard he mustered his Para troop. He designated as his second in command one Gala Freedee, older than he and greatly experienced. They then took to the Duke's stables, smelling of horse scents and sounding of neigh sayers. Mounted, they crossed the courtyard, left the road and entered the tall, wind blown grasses of the Duke's eastern hill lands. Clop clop, clippity clip, clip, trumph, trumph, thurumph, they rode.

They hadn't traveled far before night began to fall and Firstyr called a halt to make camp. Gala Freedee approached the young knight as he squatted before the campfire, stirring its flames with a stick, just as the thoughts of the coming challenges stirred in his mind.

"I know the Allusion, Sir Firstyr," she said, "I, myself, worked on the Duke's easement . . . in my younger days . . . before the Legalese." She swept some ground with the toe of her boot, and then squatted beside the knight. "Simpler times, lord. The passage was roughly hewn and plowed through the swampland, without plotted course or design, and was easily lost to travelers even then. But, Warefors and Hirtafors did not roam the swamp then. The Legalese were not afoot. It is very dangerous, now."

"And," she continued, "there is rumor of a wizard! A Wordlock, who miscasts phrases and misspells, and creates confusion such as to cause vagueness and uncertainty where none should exist. If the Lady Lawra and her company came under his spell, then they might never be found. They would be lost as surely as if in the grasp of the Legalese." She glanced with concern at the knight, and continued. "While the Paras are brave and true, and you yourself are renowned for strength and cunning, I am not sure what we few can do, if the Wordlock is allied with the Legalese."

The knight continued to stir the fire as he heard and considered this counsel. He understood how travelers might become lost in the Allusion, even in simpler times, especially while attempting to follow a vaguely defined passageway. The added threat of the Legalese and their alliance with a Wordlock caused his consternation to bead in perspiration upon his brow.

He stood. "Perhaps we are not enough," he said to Gala Freedee. "I bid you to go south . . . to the land of Cort. There is a magician there, one Pandolphe. Find him and plead that he returns with you to me, to aid us in this trial. Although he owes me nothing, and there is danger here without reward, he may nevertheless accept the challenge of battling a famous wizard such as the Wordlock. Leave now, before sunrise. We will continue on shortly after dawn. As there will be but two of you and you will be traveling light, you should reach us just as we prepare to enter the Allusion."

"As you wish," said Gala Freedee. She turned away, mounted her pony and, with the dig of her stirrup and a hearty hie ho, she hastened to her task, quickly disappearing in the darkness.

Although exhausted from the day's events, the knight could not thereafter sleep. He tossed and turned in his blanket on the ground, his normally brave composure tested by the imagined perils of the coming trial and the uncertainty of Gala's mission. With the first break of light he arose and rousted the Paras to readiness.

They quickly mounted and were on their way. They traveled towards the horizon at the sun's pace, stopping only to allow the Paras to reload their selectrics. Shortly after nightfall they reached the edge of the Allusion, where, to their surprise, Gala Freedee awaited them with a ready campfire. With her was the magician, Pandolphe, dressed in green mechanic's coveralls.

The knight and Gala Freedee made high fives in salutation. Then Firstyr turned to the magician. "I am most grateful that you have come," he said. "We are greatly tasked, and I fear that the challenge might only be met with your skillful artifice."

There was a twinkle in the magician's eye, and a smile dimpled his cheek. "It is not artifice, young knight," he said, "but, the art of persuasion. Have not the soothsaying readers of tealeaves prescribed: 'Believe not what the leaves may say, unless persuasion doth win the day?' And, does not a judge verily rebut black letter law by decreeing that the burden of persuasion has not been met? *Onus persuadere!*"

"Will you help us?" Gala Freedee asked the magician. Whereupon Firstyr pulled the map of the easement from his breast pocket and presented it to Pandolphe. The magician unfolded the yellowed Mylar and studied the drawing. He looked at the knight quizzically. "Is there a grant of right?" he asked.

"Only this runic deed," replied the knight as he handed the magician a rolled and ribboned parchment.

"An Allusion illusion!" exclaimed the magician. "Your troubles are greater than you may have imagined," he worriedly said to the knight. "Your Duke's daughter . . . what's her name?"

"It is Lawra," answered Gala Freedee.

"Lawra," continued the magician. "If the Lady Lawra encountered a Wordlock at the edge of the Allusion, then she most assuredly is now lost in an endless maze of illusion. She may never be found. When she presumed to enter upon the right-of-way, she may have, by the wizard's trickery, entered upon a wrong way. We must hurry. I will explain further as we go." But, there would be no time for any further explanations.

They hurried, and quickly reached the edge of the dreary Allusion swamp, dark and dank. The humid air was thick and held echoing night sounds of hoot owls, bullfrogs and crickets, the rustling of leaves and the creaking of tree limbs. None among the company was truly afraid, but there was little comfort to be shared among them. Pandolphe moved forward, intending to assume the party's lead, when suddenly a blinding light burst from woods and there appeared the Wordlock in a glittering black robe.

"By what claim of right do you enter here?" demanded the Wordlock. "By what easement? Continuing . . . Discontinuing . . . Intermittent? Convenience . . . Necessity? Quasi . . . Implied? Affirmative . . . Negative? Reciprocal Negative? Gross? Appurtenant? Apparent? Equitable? Public . . . Private? What say you?" he scowled.

"You've forgotten Prescription," interrupted Pandolphe, "although that is not our sole claim. We claim all manner and type of easement that suits our purposes. And . . . we have a deed." He raised and extended the rolled parchment before him. The Paras closed ranks behind him. There were the clicks of the selectric switches. Firstyr reached for his sword.

"A deed?" laughed the haughty Wordlock. He grabbed the parchment from the magician's outstretched hand and, as he did so, a gang of Warefors and Hirtafors encircled Firstyr and his company. "The Legalese delight in dissecting deeds," he laughed. "Let us see." He unrolled the parchment.

"This grant is illusory," he sneered derisively. "There are no defined terms. The bounds of the easement commence at a weathered mere stone, but they do not return there, since the deed does not recite *'the aforesaid.'* Your easement is an illusion.

Perhaps you should try that passageway over there." He pointed to a clearing some hundred yards to the north. "It is well known that you cannot step into the same river twice," he lectured.

Firstyr whispered over Pandolphe's shoulder, "That must be the way he sent the Lady Lawra. We should hurry. Gala Freedee and the Paras can easily dispose of these Legalese."

"Hush," commanded the magician as he turned his attention back to the Wordlock.

"Discordant harmony is an oxymoron," Pandolphe replied. Lex est Logos. The deed mentions only the one weathered mere stone. Noscitur a sociis. This is elementary school grammar, Mr. *so-called* wizard. Your misspells and misconstructions will not work here, notwithstanding your forces of Legalese."

Upon hearing this, the Warefors and the Hirtafors became doubtful and confused. Firstyr saw his opportunity, and signaled the Paras to attack. With the snicks and snacks of his sword, and the blinding whiteouts flashed by the selectrics, the Legalese were scattered, leaving the Wordlock standing alone and befuddled. Pandolphe dismissed him with a wave of his hand, and the Wordlock was gone in a poof of smoke.

"To yonder clearing," commanded Firstyr, charging to the lead.

"Hold," demanded Pandolphe, raising his opened palm before him. As he did, the clearing suddenly closed, with trees, brambles and bushes seeming to magically appear out of nowhere. "The illusion is ended," he said.

"But, the maze . . . the Lady Lawra?" begged Firstyr fearfully.

"Look!" exclaimed Gala Freedee, pointing before them with a trembling hand.

There, a short distance down the path of the right-of-way appeared the Lady Lawra with her entourage, looking disheveled and bewildered, but otherwise unharmed.

"What? Where are we? Who are you?" asked the Lady Lawra before she recognized Gala Freedee. "Gala!" she exclaimed, "how come you to this place? How come we to you? We were lost and forlorn, wandering seemingly in circles for days on end. We doubted that we would ever find our way free of the Allusion. Now, here you are! Are we saved? Truly saved?"

Gala rushed forward and genuflected before the Lady Lawra, head bowed, her eyes moist with tears of joy. "By the bravery of this young knight," she said, indicating Firstyr, "and by the persuasion of this magician," she continued, but when she turned to find Pandolphe, he was not among them. "Firstyr?" she said inquiringly. But Firstyr could offer no explanation. Pandolphe had simply vanished with a poof.

The Lady Lawra approached the brave, young knight and warmly grasped both his hands. "My hero," she blushed demurely. Firstyr genuflected and placed himself unendingly in her service. "My free act and deed," he vowed.

FIRSTYR SAVES A HEAD, OR
TWINKLE, TWINKLE STARE DECISIS

Pandolphe had not wanted to leave the celebration of Lawra's rescue so quickly and unannounced, but it was important that he stay close on the trail of the Wordlock.

When wizards poof-away, they do not simply reappear at some other earthly place, like a garden or something. They go to a timeless and boundless, nearly celestial world. An evening space lit only by countless twinkling stars, some shooting brightly across a violet sky. A place called *Stare Decisis*. There the wizards may waft about or hobnob, waiting for the moment when some earthly mischief beckons, or they hear a plaintive plea for magical intercession. Mostly they will just sit around and play chess. Their favorite piece is the white pawn.

This is not to say that a wizard's time in *Stare Decisis* is not without its share of horseplay, such as wizards might, they generally being too old for much rough housing. But, now and then a couple of wizards might tussle over a patented spell or incantation, or one and another might wrestle over the meaning of some ancient runes or some other dispute. Their hats fall off when they push and shove.

Although Pandolphe had bested the Wordlock at the Allusion Swamp, he still had a score to settle, and he arrived in *Stare Decisis* fixing for a tussle. Of course, disputes are not settled in *Stare Decisis* by fisticuffs, but by resort to the yellowed and dog-eared volumes of ancient wizard lore and dogma. Nevertheless, Pandolphe was in a fighting mood because the scheming Wordlock had put him in a real pickle.

You see, Pandolphe's last mischief in Cort had exposed King Meenot to a good deal of embarrassment and ridicule. Even some members of the Council of Peal would gleefully but quietly snicker whenever the King passed through the halls. So, the King was real mad, and in a peevish mood he demanded Pandolphe's head.

However, the law in Cort was quite clear on this subject. You could not lop off a man's head just because he had caused the King some embarrassment. First, there was the matter of free speech and all that. But, more importantly, the people of Cort enjoyed a good laugh now and then, and the best laughs always came at the expense of the nobility. That being the case, a good laugh at the expense of a King could never be a capital offense and this was black letter law in Cort, to King Meenot's chagrin.

Whereupon entered the Wordlock. He instructed the King that just because the law clearly said what it meant, that did not always mean that the law meant what it said.

This perplexed the King, but he was willing to listen further. Had I not mentioned earlier that the King was not too bright?

"I have invited some statutory construction workers over from the Legalese," said the Wordlock. "They have studied the old cases and the legislative history of this law. Although the law says that a *man* shall not lose his head for poking fun at the King, it is quite clear that the law was enacted to protect *court jesters*."

"Therefore, it is well reasoned," he continued, "that the law affords Pandolphe no protection. The court jester is a man. Pandolphe is not the court jester. Therefore, Pandolphe is not a man. Ipso facto, your Highness may have Pandolphe's head!"

The King was dozing, which was his propensity during legal arguments; but, with the mention of "Pandolphe's head" he woke straight up with a snort. "What's that you say? I can have Pandolphe's head! Let the word go out to my sheriffs. Bring me the head of Pandolphe!" the King commanded.

Fortunately, Pandolphe had left Cort shortly after the Loyalty Day Parade. Indeed, when Gala Freedee had been sent there to fetch him, she did not get that far. She found the wizard along her route, sitting under an apple tree, concocting the law of gravity. Pandolphe had been making his own way to the Allusion Swamp, being by that time already on the trail of the Wordlock. However, the trail would not this new day end in *Stare Decisis*.

The Wordlock had been alerted to Pandolphe's vengeful mood, and had decided it would be best if he settled for a while in Cort, where Pandolphe would not dare to tread.

If Pandolphe was to right the wrong done to him by the Wordlock, he would need an emissary to Cort. He turned to the brave, young knight, Firstyr the Younger.

Upon hearing Pandolphe's case, Firstyr met with Duke Senexatty. Because of his earlier banishment, he would need a safe conduct to travel to Cort, he explained. The Duke would not deny him; but, warned him to be on his guard, for even diplomatic immunity might not shield him from the King's sheriffs. Firstyr assured the Duke of his vigilance, and left for a long night among the records of past Cort tribulations. He did not sleep. When morning came he took his leave, saddled his pony and rode.

He had barely arrived in Cort when he was apprehended by mercenary Legalese and brought before the Cort Council of Peals. "Don't we know you? Weren't you once banished from this land?" gruffly inquired the Chief Councilor.

"I come under the safe conduct of Duke Senexatty of Transactional," explained the knight, "to appeal the sentence of Pandolphe the wizard."

"This should be interesting," the Chief Councilor backhandedly said to the others on the bench, and they snickered. "On what grounds would you appeal?" he asked the knight. "You of all people should know that we will not retry the facts," he said. "And," he added, "while there may have been some question of the law, we found Pandolphe to be an exception." The snickering on the bench grew louder.

"Honorable Council," the knight began, "the exception tests the rule. The law of Cort for centuries, affirmed in numerous decisions of this Council, prohibits a sentence so extreme. It is an unusual punishment and exceedingly cruel, but more than that it is against the rule. As this Council once lectured me, when last I was here, security and certainty are held very dear. Precedent, then, should carry the day, and Pandolphe's sentence this Council should stay."

"We find your rhymes amusing," the Chief Councilor chuckled, "but your whimsy cannot overcome the logic of the Wordlock, and precedent must yield when necessary to vindicate a right."

"But, by the Wordlock's logic," the knight replied, "the King, himself, would not be a man, for the King also is not the court jester. But, as we all had ample opportunity to observe at the Loyalty Day Parade, the King most certainly is a man."

There followed some commotion at the bench, and some unexplained guffaws. This awoke the dozing King, who didn't understand the fluttered wink that one councilor threw his way. Quiet was demanded, and the Chief Councilor turned his attention back to Firstyr.

"Young knight," he said, "you obviously have gained much wisdom during your exile. I admit, too, that your brave adventures are not unknown to us. You have convinced us, or at least a majority, that an error has been made. Pandolphe may keep his head. And you, young knight, shall once again be welcomed in Cort."

Bells rang in the Cort towers that day, and more bells welcomed Firstyr on his return to the Duke's castle. Soon there would be wedding bells, as the young knight and the Lady Lawra exchanged their marriage vows. They would live happily ever after.

Back in *Stare Decisis*, Pandolphe knocked the Wordlock's hat off.

THE BAILIFF AND STENOGRAPHER
OR THE PEREMTORY CHALLENGE

The judge is sitting at his bench,
As sitting is his right.
The jury weighs the evidence,
As is their ancient plight.
And this we're assured is providence,
Because dame justice has no sight.

The defendant sits impatiently,
Hoping the jury will be fair.
His lawyer fiddles nervously
With her papers, pens or hair.
But, the bailiff and stenographer, they
Hardly have a care.

The bailiff and stenographer,
They've seen it many times.
From philanderer to pornographer,
From high to petty crimes.
At recess they go off together
And drink their gin with limes.

They hurry back before one o'clock
None the worse for wear.
They take their place beside the dock
Just below the judge's chair.
They give attention at the gavel's knock
But, they avoid the judge's stare.

The judge harrumphs to clear his throat
And the defendant's asked to plead.
The stenographer takes cryptic notes
That only she can read.
The bailiff polls the jury's vote
But only eleven are agreed.

The twelfth has doubt,
He tells the court.
The judge sends the others out.
"This trial I will not abort,
So what's this all about?
Please try to make it short."

The juror is firm as he declares
"I think he's innocent."
The gallery awakes with wide-eyed stares
At the juror's impertinence.
"Does he deny that this trial was fair,
After all of the time we've spent?"

"The fingerprints are not this man's
A simple test could plainly tell.
And what are the modus operands
If the gun's not his as well?"
The stenographer did not understand
The words she could not spell.

The bailiff cried "oyer, oyer!"
As the gallery went wild.
The judge told the juror to reconfer
And to try to be reconciled.
The lawyers asked of one another,
"What appeals must now be filed?"

Back inside the jury room
The twelfth juror did continue,
\"You'd send this poor man to his doom
But this court has not the venue.
This man's guilt you'd just presume
Although fair process he is due."

"That is what the Articles say,
And Amendments four and five.
A man in court should have his day,
Before his freedom you deprive.
You cannot convict him in your way.
At least not while I'm alive!"

The bailiff and stenographer
In the courtroom patiently waited.
The jury returned by the back door
Their faces elongated.
The judge called the court to order.
The gallery held its breath abated.

The tower clock began to toll.
The time was half past seven.
The bailiff began the jury poll,
But he counted only eleven.
"Where's the twelfth?" he wanted to know.
The foreman pointed to heaven.

"We tried to make him see our way
But, he simply would not budge.
He fought with us throughout the day,
But, we should not hold a grudge.
For his dear soul we ought to pray,"
The foreman told the judge.

The judge tried to make some sense
Of what was being said.
On the basis of this evidence
He presumed the juror dead.
The foreman's glare was so intense,
That the judge just shook his head.

"Poll the eleven," the judge directed,
And the bailiff did as he was told.
Thus the defendant was convicted,
And imprisoned until he was old.
The stenography was then corrected
And, thus was justice sold.

The bailiff and stenographer
Left the courtroom hand in hand.
They had seen this all before . . .
The conviction of an innocent man.
And of one thing they could be sure,
They would see it again and again.

So you lawyers and you liberal types
Who contemplate the 'what ifs?'
Beware of the due process hypes
As defendants or as plaintiffs
And heed this verse that I recite
Of stenographers and bailiffs.

PETER AND PAUL[1]
THE HOLDER IN DUE COURSE

'Peter is poor,' said noble Paul,
   'And I have always been his friend:
And, though my means to give are small,
   At least I can afford to lend.
How few, in this cold age of greed,
   Do good, except on selfish grounds!
But I can feel for Peter's need,
   And I WILL LEND HIM FIFTY POUNDS!'

        How great was Peter's joy to find
           His friend in such a genial vein!
        How cheerfully the bond he signed,
           To pay the money back again!
        'We can't,' said Paul, 'be too precise:
           'Tis best to fix the very day:
        So, by a learned friend's advice,
           I've made Noon, the Fourth of May'

'But this is April' Peter said.
  'The First of April, as I think.
Five little weeks will soon be fled:
  One scarcely will have time to wink!
Give me a year to speculate –
  To buy and sell – to drive a trade –'
Said Paul, 'I cannot change the date.
  On May the Fourth it must be paid.'

'Well, well!' said Peter, with a sigh.
  'Hand me the cash, and I will go.
I'll form a Joint-Stock Company,
  And turn an honest pound or so.'
'I'm grieved,' said Paul, 'to seem unkind:
  The money shall of course be lent:
But, for a week or two, I find
  It will not be convenient.'

So, week-by-week, poor Peter came
  And turned in heaviness away;
For still the answer was the same,
  'I cannot manage it to-day.'
And now the April showers were dry –
  The five short weeks were nearly spent –
Yet still he got the old reply,
  'It is not quite convenient!'

The Fourth arrived, and punctual Paul
  Came, with his legal friend, at noon:
'I thought it best,' said he, 'to call:
  One cannot settle things too soon.'
Poor Peter shuddered in despair:
  His flowing locks he wildly tore:
And very soon his yellow hair
  Was lying all about the floor.

The legal friend was standing by,
  With sudden pity half unmanned:
The teardrop trembled in his eye,
  The signed agreement in his hand:
But when at length the legal soul
  Resumed its customary force,
'The Law,' he said, 'we can't control:
  Pay, or the Law must take its course!'

Said Paul 'How bitterly I rue
   That fatal morning when I called!
Consider, Peter, what you do!
   You won't be richer when you're bald!
Think you, by rending curls away,
   To make your difficulties less?
Forbear this violence, I pray:
   You do but add to my distress!'

'Not willingly would I inflict,'
   Said Peter, 'on that noble heart
One needless pang. Yet why so strict?
   Is this to act a friendly part?
However legal it may be
   To pay what never has been lent,
This style of business seems to me
   Extremely inconvenient!

'No Nobleness of soul have I,
   Like some that in this Age are found!
(Paul blushed in sheer humility,
   And cast his eyes upon the ground.)
'This debt will simply swallow all,
   And make my life a life of woe!'
'Nay, nay, my Peter!' answered Paul.
   'You must not rail on Fortune so!

'You have enough to eat and drink:
   You are respected in the world:
And at the barber's, as I think,
   You often get your whiskers curled.
Though Nobleness you can't attain –
   To any very great extent –
The path of Honesty is plain
   However inconvenient!'

''Tis true,' said Peter, 'I'm alive:
   I keep my station in the world:
Once in the week I just contrive
   To get my whiskers oiled and curled.
But my assets are very low:
   My little income's overspent:
To trench on capital, you know,
   Is always inconvenient!'

'But pay your debts!' cried honest Paul
  'My gentle Peter, pay your debts!
What matter if it swallows all
  That you describe as your 'assets'?
    Already you're an hour behind:
Yet Generosity is best.
    It pinches me – but never mind!
I WILL NOT CHARGE YOU INTEREST!'

'How good! How great!' poor Peter cried.
  'Yet I must sell my Sunday wig –
The scarf-pin that has been my pride –
  My grand piano – and my pig!'
Full soon his property took wing:
  And daily, as each treasure went,
He sighed to find the state of things
  Grow less and less convenient.

Weeks grew to months, and months to years:
  Peter was worn to skin and bone:
And once he even said, with tears,
  'Remember, Paul, that promised loan!'
Said Paul 'I'll lend you, when I can,
  All the spare money I have got –
Ah, Peter, you're a happy man!
  Yours is an enviable lot!

'I'm getting stout, as you may see;
  It is but seldom I am well:
I cannot feel my ancient glee
  In listening to the dinner-bell:
But you, you gambol like a boy,
  Your figure is so spare and light;
The dinner bell's a note of joy
  To such a healthy appetite!'

Said Peter 'I am well aware
  Mine is a state of happiness:
And yet how gladly could I spare
Some of the comforts I possess!
What you call healthy appetite
  I feel as Hunger's savage tooth:
And, when no dinner is in sight,
  The dinner bell's a sound of Ruth!

'No scare-crow would accept this coat;
    Such boots as these you seldom see,
Ah, Paul, a single five-pound-note
    Would make another man of me!'
Said Paul 'It fills me with surprise
    To hear you talk in such a tone:
I fear you scarcely realize
    The blessings that are all your own!

'You're safe from being overfed:
    You're sweetly picturesque in rags:
You never know the aching head
    That comes along with moneybags:
And you have time to cultivate
    That best of qualities, Content —
For which you'll find your present state
    Remarkably convenient!
Said Peter 'Though I cannot sound
    The depths of such a man as you,
Yet in your character I've found
    An inconsistency or two.
You seem to have long years to spare
    When there's a promise to fulfill:
And yet how punctual you were
    In calling with that little bill!'

'One can't be too deliberate,'
    Said Paul, 'in parting with one's pelf.
With bills, as you correctly state,
    I'm punctuality itself.
A man may surely claim his dues:
    But, when there's money to be lent,
A man must be allowed to choose
    Such times as are convenient!'

It chanced one day, as Peter sat
    Gnawing a crust — his usual meal —
Paul bustled in to have a chat,
    And grasped his hand with friendly zeal.
'I knew,' said he, 'your frugal ways:
    So, that I might not wound your pride
By bringing strangers to gaze,
    I've left my legal friend outside!

'You well remember, I am sure,
When first your wealth began to go,
    And people sneered at one so poor,
I never used my Peter so!
    And when you'd lost your little all
And found yourself a thing despised,
    I need not ask you to recall
How tenderly I sympathized!

'Then the advice I've poured on you,
    So full of wisdom and of wit:
All given gratis, though 'tis true
    I might have fairly charged for it!
But I refrain from mentioning
    Full many a deed I might relate –
For boasting is a kind of thing
    That I particularly hate.

'How vast the total sum appears
    Of all the kindnesses I've done,
From Childhood's half-forgotten years
    Down to that Loan of April One!
That Fifty Pounds! You little guessed
    How deep it drained my slender store:
But there's a heart within this breast,
And I WILL LEND YOU FIFTY MORE!'

'Not so,' was Peter's mild reply,
    His cheeks all wet with grateful tears:
'No man recalls, so well as I,
    Your services in bygone years:
And this new offer, I admit,
    Is very very kindly meant –
Still to avail myself of it
    Would not be quite convenient!"

EPILOGUE

I imagine that you now probably have one last question, which is: Why is the white pawn the wizard's favorite chess piece? That's because the white pawn always makes the first move to capture the king. Good night and pleasant dreams.

Printed in the United States
By Bookmasters